MW00619710

MOMMY LOVES YOU

Written and Illustrated by
Lois Kim

WATERMARK
PUBLISHING

ISBN: 978-1-935690-95-5

Library of Congress Control Number: 2017953299

Design and Production
Dawn Sakamoto Paiva

Watermark Publishing
1000 Bishop Street, Suite 806
Honolulu, HI 96813
Telephone (toll-free): 1-866-900-BOOK
www.bookshawaii.net

Printed in Korea

*This book is dedicated to my beautiful daughter, Ashley Yuri Kim,
and my spirited son, Josiah Yoo Chun Berry.
Even though Mommy had to go away, remember, I still love you.*

Illustration by Ashley Yuri Kim

No matter how far or how long,
this statement will never be wrong:
Mommy loves you!

Some mommies have to go away
for different reasons.
Some mommies have to go away
for different lengths of time.

But no matter how far or how long,
this statement will never be wrong:
Mommy loves you!

Some mommies go because
they have things to do.

Others have people to meet,
and still others just want time
for themselves.

Relax
Spa
-Waxing
-Acrylic
- Highlights
- lowlights
- Aroma
Therapy
25%
OFF
FOR
MOM!

Some mommies go to
the grocery store.

SALE
A 10 B
$2.10/lb
ORANGE ORANGES

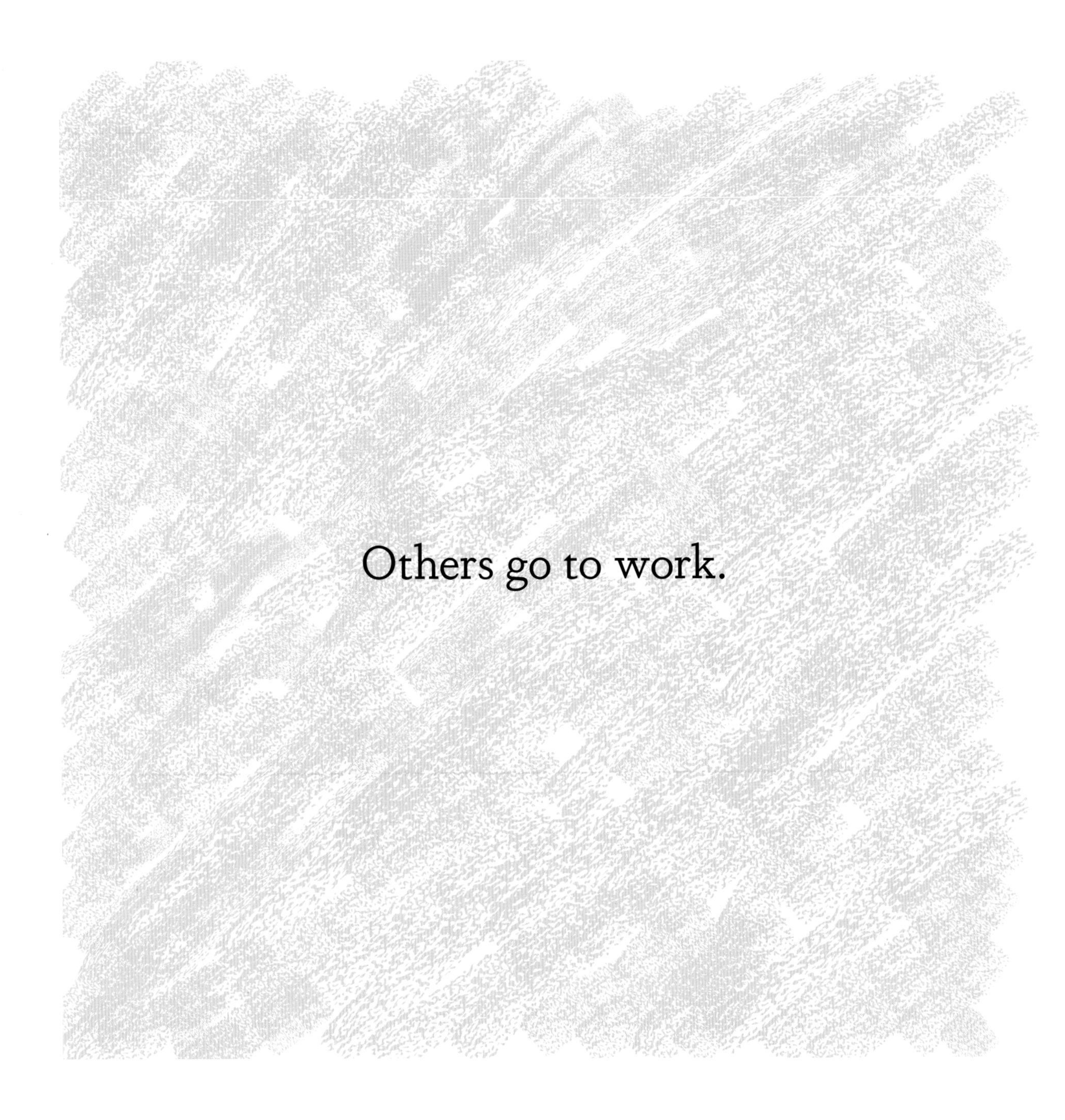

Others go to work.

And still others go on trips.

But no matter how far or how long,
this statement will never be wrong:

Mommy loves you!

Some mommies are gone for
just a few minutes,
others a few days.

And others are gone forever.

IN
LOVING
MEMORY

Some mommies go for breaks,
some for time outs.

And still some become angels.

But no matter how long,
or for what reason
mommies are gone,

Always remember one thing . . .

MOMMY LOVES YOU.

I ♥ U

Acknowledgments

I would like to thank Read To Me International for giving me a voice when I assumed silence was my only option and YWCA Oʻahu for being a beacon of light during my darkest days. Without these two organizations, my dreams would never have become realities.

Thank you from the bottom of my heart.

—Lois Kim

To learn more about the work these two local organizations do to support our community, please visit www.readtomeintl.org and www.ywcaoahu.org.